Ann Jonas
Where Can It Be?

Greenwillow Books/New York

To Amy, who inspired this book,
and to Nina, who helped create it.

Printed in Japan by
Dai Nippon Printing Co.
First Edition
10 9 8 7 6 5 4 3 2 1

Library of Congress
Cataloging-in-Publication Data
Jonas, Ann.   Where can it be?
Summary: A child looks all over
the house for her missing blanket.
[1. Lost and found possessions
—Fiction]   I. Title.
PZ7.J664Wi 1986   [E]   86-304
ISBN 0-688-05169-3
ISBN 0-688-05246-0 (lib. bdg.)

Watercolor paints and colored pencils
were used for the full-color art.
The typeface is Helvetica Bold.

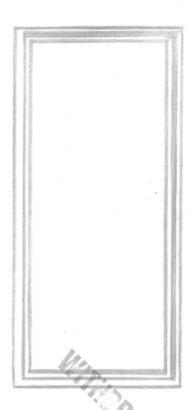

I don't know
where I left it.
I'm sure I brought it
home with me.
I have to find it!

I'll look in my closet!

Just my clothes.

**I'll look in
my cupboard!**

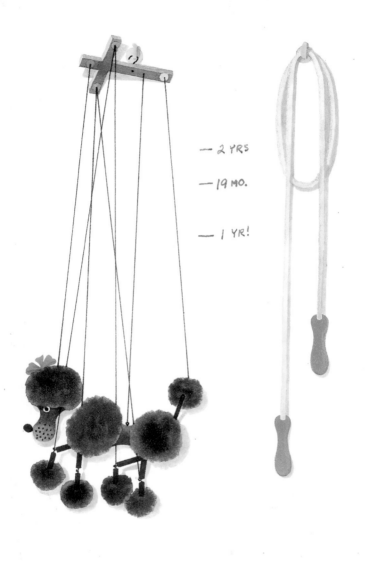

— 2 YRS

— 19 MO.

— 1 YR!

Just my toys.

Just my cat.

I'll look in the kitchen!

Just pots.

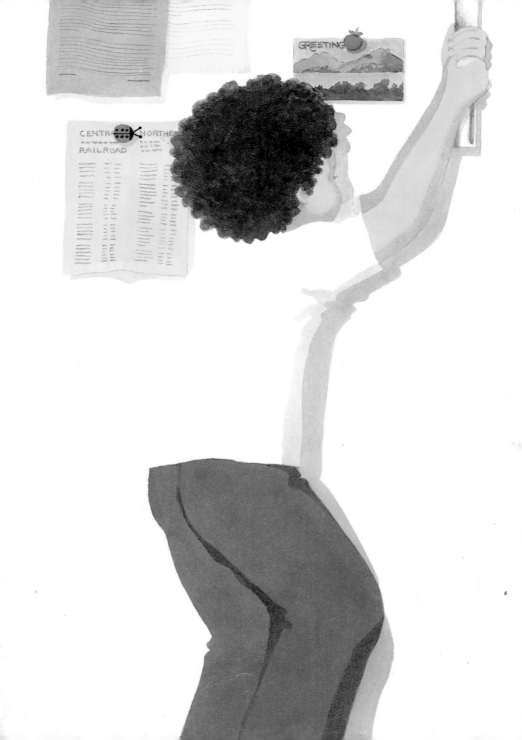

Just cold food.

I'll look under the table!

Just my cat again.

**Maybe I left it
at Deborah's house.
The doorbell is ringing.**

780

LETTERS

It's Deborah and

my blanket!